Murder

in

Queen's Park

By Tim Lewis

Also by Tim Lewis:

Murder in Belgrave Square
Murder in Dartmouth Park

The rest of the series, coming soon:
Murder on the Docks
A Killer in the House

ISBN 10: 09863052-5-1

ISBN 13: 978-0-9863052-5-2

Cover by David Prendergast

Editor: Kymberlie Ingalls

Scotland Yard Detective Edward Willoughby and his team of police officers are pursuing contract assassin Ronald Alexander. He has already killed three people, all related to a garment factory fire seven years past. Despite Scotland Yard's best efforts, the killer is still at large.

And he has an agenda:

The Garment Factory Principles (Targets):

- o The Principle Owners:
  - Langley Smythe (principle, 76%)
  - Harley Winthorpe (principle, 13%)
  - Harold Lawton (principle 7%)
  - ~~Luella Walford aka Lady Manchester~~ (principle, 4%) - In Prison
    - Arrested for the Murder of her husband, and for hiring a contract killer to murder his mistress.
- o Management:
  - ~~John Connelly~~ - Deceased
  - Janet Englert
  - Reginald Naughton
  - ~~Neville Anderson~~ – Deceased

One

"I want him dead." The gentleman's breath was icy, coming out in clouds in the late night London fog. "Public and brutal." He pulled his top hat down a bit tighter. His bespoke suit screamed wealth, even in the dim light.

"As you wish, m'lord." Lifeless eyes studied the man who was hiring him. His newsboy hat shadowed his indistinct face.

Carleton "Abbs" Abby watched from his cover of the shrubbery in the park. He rubbed his bleary eyes, trying desperately to sober up. What he was hearing jolted him to the core: a murder being planned? The wharf rat leaned forward, his ears straining to hear the details. His filthy clothes were dark, protecting him from being discovered.

"Detective Willoughby has taken down far too much of my organization," the well-dressed man continued. "It must be done soon."

"I'll have the bugger on a slab in a week, possibly less."

"Less time will get you more money."

"Will contact you when I'm done." The man with the lifeless eyes disappeared into the fog.

* * * * *

The well-heeled man shivered as he turned to walk toward the south end of Queen's Park. Abbs watched a third man emerge from the shadows and gain on him. The gentleman looked down as he walked. His hands were jammed into his pockets, a red wool scarf wrapped around his neck.

Two powerful hands pulled the scarf to the rear. The gentleman attempted to reach behind him, but was dragged into the flowerbeds, his hands flailing. They only caught air.

Abbs stifled a gasp, and watched with eyes wide open. Seconds ticked by. The gentleman's arms hung limp at his sides, offering no resistance. A blade glinted in the dim glow of the gas street lamps. A left hand swiped the throat, and blood spewed down the front of the man.

"For my wife," a calm voice said. He strode out of the park.

Abbs stared at the body for a few moments, trying to decide what to do. He backed up and crept away from the death before him. He stopped short of the gate when he saw a cab. The cabbie was sitting on the high perch of his two-wheeled Hansom carriage, smoking a cigarette. The dark horse snorted, and shook his head.

The hired killer with the lifeless eyes approached.

"Ready, sir?" the cabbie asked, as he jumped to the ground and opened the door for his fare. The dim light revealed his leather boilerman's cap.

"More than ready," the killer replied, stepping toward the door. His hand reached for the boarding handle. A thin blade sliced his neck.

It's 'im, Abbs thought, clamping his mouth shut with both hands. *It's the ghost.* Heart thumping, he backed into the park, the dark shielding him once more.

The killer clutched his neck in a futile attempt to stop the bleeding. The cabbie spun the man away from the carriage, and blood splattered onto the walk.

"I cannot allow you to kill the detective," the cabbie whispered as the body slumped against the spokes of the wheel.

Abbs withdrew to the relative safety of the park, sitting in the thick brush until he was certain the ghost/cabbie was gone.

* * * * *

A bobby strode down Harrow Lane, the wall of Kensal Green Cemetery looming to his right. He rounded the gradual turn, revealing the Anglican Chapel. The policeman stopped. It was deathly silent. The fog blew in clouds across the entrance, partially obscuring the details.

Night after night he had noted the church steps until they were as familiar as his own flat. The grey came and went, fast and slow: caressing, holding, then abandoning the structure.

"Is that what I think it is?" the constable muttered to himself. He could just identify something—or someone— on the porch of the ancient church.

He approached the Georgian columns. Two bodies hung from the ceiling of the chapel. The patrolman lit his lantern and shined it at the corpses.

"Mother of God!" he exclaimed.

Blood covered the front of both men. Each body had a paper sign pinned to their lapel. One fellow was labeled 'Murderer', while the other's sign said 'Killer'."

A third note fluttered on the pant leg of one of the men: "Police: contact Edward Willoughby, Scotland Yard." He scratched his head, and pulled his whistle. He blew hard, summoning every copper within earshot.

Two

Edward Willoughby paced and sipped his tea. He set the cup on the elegant saucer and took a bite from his biscuit. The clock ticked loudly, reminding him it was after two in the morning and he needed sleep.

He continued to think of the events of recent weeks, pondering what direction to take. Three bodies in the morgue, more than a hundred people rescued from an underground hell, and there were more questions than answers.

The living room demonstrated a neatness Edward Willoughby did not naturally possess. His late, great aunt had last organized and cleaned it seven years earlier. With her passing, he inherited the residence. Thank God for Mrs. Haggersly: she kept it almost as clean as Marguerite Willoughby.

He shuffled into the study and wrote on a blackboard jammed with notes and scrawls. Many scraps of paper crowded a corkboard.

Documents and journals filled the small room of the Kensington residence. File folders from Scotland Yard—detailing crimes as far back as several decades—occupied the bottoms of the piles, while unfiled details from current crimes graced the peaks of the paper mountains.

Photographs: bodies and crime scenes. An attractive young woman with her throat slit bothering Edward the most: an innocent victim of an unsolved murder.

Newspaper clippings: Most of them detailed the garment factory fires, seven years earlier. Almost 200 women had died.

Notes: Copied from journals, some from constables, and some from the journals and letters of victims of crimes.

Edward sat in his easy chair and began to nod off.

* * * * *

The screams. He could still hear the women's screams. They were dying, and hundreds of voices created their own dirge.

Bells clanged, police whistles howled into the dingy night: chaos was everywhere. The low clouds and fog turned pink from the flames.

"We've got to get 'em out!" The black-stained face of the constable looked through the rain at the smoldering building. "There's hunnerds of women in there!" His hands were scorched and bleeding. The uniformed policeman turned to run into the building when Edward grabbed him from behind, wrapping both his arms around the big man.

"You will do no one any good if you perish in the flames yourself, man," Edward breathed into his ear. "Be logical. We make a plan. Then we go get them together."

Firemen wielded hoses, climbed ladders to the upper floors of the brick building. They used their axes to break through the iron gratings, which sealed the windows and doors.

"Willoughby, Scotland Yard, chief," Edward shouted at a senior fireman. "How can we be of assistance?"

"Stretcher bearers, detective," the intense eyes bore through Edward. Rain poured off the helmet of the burly man. "Get the injured clear. Find a store, restaurant, anything. Get 'em out of this weather."

"Will do. Stay with me constable. We have our task." He released the bobby, a dazed look about him. Rain poured from Edward's bowler as he turned to a handful of detectives arriving from Scotland Yard. "Sam, find a café, restaurant, or some other such place to get the victims out of the rain. The rest of you, follow me." They all hesitated.

"Well don't just stand there with your fingers in your arses," Sam barked. "Follow Detective Willoughby.

Now." He tipped his dripping hat at Edward. "I'll clear out the Bull and Castle and be awaitin' for ye." He marched his huge body toward the corner pub. By the time the first stretchers arrived, the bar was cleared of patrons and the tables were ready to receive patients. Sam's rotund body served as both gate guard and keeper.

The constable and Edward forced the stretcher with a young girl through the door. Tiny, blackened fingers reached for Edward's, then fell to the sheet. He took the hand and looked into the young girl's eyes. She was dead already.

* * * * *

Edward started, and shook himself awake.

Same dream, he thought. His shaking hands wiped his sweat-covered forehead. He dried his fingers on his trousers and checked if the soot was still on his palms.

A sharp rap from the knocker on his front door caused him to spill a tiny bit of his tepid black tea onto the saucer. He set his china down carefully, walked toward the door, and looked through the peephole. A uniformed policeman blew into his hands and stomped his feet. A growler carriage waited on the street. He opened the door.

"Detective Edward Willoughby?" the officer inquired.

"I am Willoughby."

"A note from Superintendent McCarthy." He handed an envelope to Edward.

"Come inside, and warm up a bit," Edward said. He returned to his chair and better light. He opened the envelope and read the note:

```
Edward:
     Two dead at
Kensal Green
Cemetery. Note for
you on one of the
bodies. Proceed with
all haste.
```

--McCarthy,
Superintendent

"Has my team been notified?" Edward asked.

"Yessir, they have. They'll arrive shortly."

"Then there is no time to waste," Edward took his cup to the kitchen, took a final sip and drained the remaining tea into the scullery. He marched toward the front door and grabbed his coat, scarf, hat, and gloves.

Edward locked his front door and turned toward the horse-drawn carriage, swinging his coat onto his shoulders.

Kensal Green Cemetery, 0311:

Cadet Peterson was the first member of Willoughby's team onsite, and took charge of the scene. The twenty-year-old kept everyone back, including two sergeants, who wanted a look-see at the crime. The young man stood like a charged lion, keeping the senior officers from the cemetery.

"Cadet Peterson, how goes it?" Edward said.

"I'll tell you how it goes detective," a gnarled sergeant said. "This cadet has over-stepped his authority, keeping me from my own crime scene."

"Keep your wig on, Sergeant," Edward said. "First, the instant the note was left for Detective Edward Willoughby of Scotland Yard, it became Scotland Yard's Crime Scene. Second, Cadet Peterson is acting on my instructions."

Edward tamped his pipe and lit it. He took a puff and let out a small cloud, surrounding his face. He fanned the smoke and continued.

"Sorry, I'm forgetting my manners. Edward Willoughby, Scotland Yard." Edward shook hands with the sergeant.

"*You're* Willoughby? My apologies. Sergeant Stevenson, Southall Station."

"Pleased to meet you, Stevenson. These are serious times and crimes. We need to contain an arena which may encompass the whole of London. I appreciate you wanting to get moving with the investigation, but there are certain aspects of these crimes to which only a few are privy. The good news is we will be doing most of the work, while crediting Southall Station with all the support."

"*All* the support?" The sergeant raised an eyebrow.

"*All* the support." Edward said. "Now sir, if you will be so kind, I see the rest of my team is arriving. Come along, Peterson."

Three

"Have you been briefed?" Edward asked as Foot Patrolman Robert Andreason exited the cab.

"Not yet. Do we have the first responders available?"

"Yes. He's over there, awaiting our interrogation." Edward pointed to a concrete bench near the two bodies.

Another cadet and two plain-clothed detectives walked up to Edward and Robert. Edward gathered his team about him, and motioned for the two sergeants to join the circle.

"If this goes as the earlier murders, this is not the crime scene, but rather a place for the police to quickly find the bodies. Sergeants Ambrose and Stevenson, could you brief your next shifts to look for a secluded area, say an alley or a park, for two large blood pools?"

Both the sergeants nodded, and everyone took notes.

"As this case," Edward continued "and yes, we are still calling it one complex case, proceeds, we may find at least one of the victims to be of some wealth or influence. Because of that possibility, we need to keep all the details under wraps. What you can tell your patrolmen is two men were murdered near Kensal Green Cemetery.

"The crime scene will be no farther than two miles from the chapel. It was foggy this night past, so an open space would have offered its own seclusion. If there is a little-used open area, *that* may be our crime scene.

"Questions, anyone?" Edward scanned the group, especially concentrating on the two sergeants.

"What about the two bodies?" Sergeant Ambrose asked.

"We have to wait for Coroner Waddington, I'm afraid," Edward said. "We may check the pockets of the victims to ascertain their identities. Once that is achieved, we can proceed no further. The coroner will have our guts for breakfast if we greatly disturb the evidence."

"I see," Sergeant Stevenson said. "I have had the privilege of meeting the coroner, and I agree we should disturb as little as possible."

Horses clomping on the cobblestone street came closer, and the coroner's wagon emerged from the fog. Two men in white greatcoats rode atop the vehicle as it slowed to a stop in front of the cemetery. The rear door opened and the slight figure of a third man.

"Ah, Coroner Waddington," Edward said. "I was bringing Southall Station up to speed. I'm afraid we've just arrived ourselves and have dispensed with the preliminaries."

"Edward, what do you have?" Waddington blew his nose into a well-used handkerchief.

"Robert, Lawrence, Franklin," Edward began. "Begin the external investigation while I brief the coroner. We'll be along shortly. Sir? I can brief you as we walk."

"Very well," Waddington wiped his nose for the third time.

"This might help, sir." Edward handed him a clean handkerchief.

"Thank you." He blew his dripping nose.

"Now, as to the information we have, it is mostly superficial…" Edward gave the coroner all the details he had by the time they were standing in front of the chapel. Waddington's two assistants trailed behind, carrying stretchers for the two bodies.

"Similar to Dartmouth Park and Highgate," Lawrence said, the large detective dusting off his knees. "Murder was elsewhere. The difference here was the signs are hand-written. I believe our killer was in a hurry. A crime of opportunity?"

"Possibly, but..." Edward said.

"But, the man labeled 'Killer' is not unknown to me."

"Go on," Edward and Waddington said together. Lawrence smiled.

"I pinched the bugger a couple of years ago as a contract killer." Lawrence pulled the collar up on his jacket. "Never put enough evidence together for a conviction, though. Wilford Davis. A-K-A 'Little Willy'. The word I got from the street is he doesn't work much, but charges a bloody fortune when he does."

"What's his signature?" Edward asked.

"He's a shooter. From a good distance, usually a hundred yards or more." Lawrence closed his eyes, referring to mental notes. "Oh, the kill is public, in broad daylight. One shot to the head, then our man is gone."

"He's that accurate?" Waddington said.

"Yes." Lawrence replied. "I still have the case files at my desk. I'll bring them over when we return to Scotland Yard."

"Thank you Lawrence. Now as to who he was contracted to kill..."

"You'd better look at the other gent, Edward," Lawrence said.

Edward walked to the chapel and looked at the overall scene to get a perspective, then he strode to the two bodies. The one labeled "Murderer" was on the left, with the note on the pant leg. He looked up at the face and paused.

"Harold Lawton," Edward breathed out, before he even thought about it. "Who were you going to kill?"

"Franklin and I are going to retrieve our weapons at The Yard, Edward," Lawrence said. "If I were Harold Lawton, and I was going to off someone, it would be one Detective Edward Willoughby."

"Edward, do you still have your Bull Dog?" Coroner Waddington said.

"Yes, sir, but my revolver would be no good against a rifle." Edward raised an eyebrow.

"They may not always try with a long weapon," the coroner said.

"Back to this investigation. Why would Ronald Alexander intervene on my behalf? Why would he even know?"

"Perhaps Ronald declined the contract," Cadet Brown said. "He obviously wants to keep you alive, sir."

"I can see Harold Lawton being caught unawares," Edward said. "But a killer for hire? I doubt he would be an easy man to take down."

"Someone familiar?" Franklin said. "Someone you would never expect to be violent."

"At two in the morning?" Edward said. "You would suspect everyone would have a certain level of malevolence."

"Let us ponder those questions later gentlemen," Coroner Waddington said, wiping his nose again. "Are you finished with the two bodies? It's a bit cold, don't you think?"

"Quite right," Edward said, standing a bit taller and buttoning his coat up to the top. "Coroner Waddington, we are finished with the bodies, but I have one question. There is a tiny bit of blood on the walk beneath each of them. So, unlike the High Gate murder, it seems these two bodies were positioned more hastily than John Connelly's was."

"Possibly, Edward," the short medical examiner said. "I'll know more once I examine them at my facility."

"Thank you sir," Edward said. "In that case, the bodies are yours."

* * * * *

Officer Andreason supervised the two cadets in evaluating the scene. Measurements were taken: How far from the street were the bodies located? Would anyone be able to easily see the person who positioned them? Was there any trace of the person who placed them here?

They scoured the immediate area for other pieces of evidence. There were no footprints, no torn piece of clothing on a bush, no spent cigarettes. Andreason followed the cadets as they walked the street in front of the cemetery, chatting as they went.

"Why here?" Peterson mused.

"I'm not sure I even understand the question," Brown said.

"The odds of being detected by the police are far greater here at the main entrance. Why not go 'round the corner to the Dissenters Gate?"

"Perhaps the odds of a beat cop noticing the bodies would be far less anywhere else in the cemetery."

"So, our killer wanted the bodies to be noticed immediately." Peterson said, tightened his wool scarf in response to a gust of wind.

"He wanted Detective Willoughby to be warned of the danger as quickly as possible?" Brown muttered.

"So, who would be the least conspicuous, here on the street?"

"A street sweeper? A copper, but all the local coppers know each other. A cabbie?" Cadet brown spun to Cadet Peterson. "A cabbie!"

They both ran back toward the crime scene. "A cabbie!" they shouted at Andreason.

* * * * *

Edward Willoughby was interviewing the first responding officers when the two cadets ran up. Edward held up his hand, ordering the young men to wait.

"So, your interval of patrol here at the cemetery is at most every half hour?" Edward wrote in his notebook.

"Yes, sir," one Bobby said. "I've never 'ad any serious crimes here in the five years I've been patrolin'. Mostly drunks trying to get home. It's the shops we patrol the most, looking for burglars and vagrants."

"Thank you officer Peyton," Edward said. "Cadets Peterson and Brown, what news have you brought?"

"Observations, Detective. Officer Peyton," Peterson began, "did ye notice any cabbies near the cemetery about the time you discovered the bodies?"

"Of course," the seasoned officer said. "I'd say a cab comes by every few minutes, any time of day or night."

"Oh." The two cadets' faces became sullen.

"On that note," Edward added, "were any of the cabbies a bit out of place? Say, too well-dressed?"

The officer thought for some time, and shrugged.

"Sorry detective. We don't note every vehicle going by, and nothing jumps out at me as being out of the ordinary."

"It's alright gents," Edward said. "If he is smart enough to steal a cab, he's smart enough to steal a cabbies' clothes. Good call, cadets. Officers, I'm going to pass this on to your sergeants, but when you return to the streets, I'd like for you to look over any cabs you encounter. These murders were messy. Surely there is some blood splattered on the wheels, or elsewhere."

"We'll be sure to look for it."

"Thank you for staying. Now go get warm somewhere."

"We'll be at Southall station, doing our paperwork if you need us." The officer tipped his hat and walked toward the street.

"Darn, I thought we had it," Peterson said.

"What you just proved is our killer is resourceful. He will adapt himself to the situation, and quite quickly." Edward smiled. "Cheer up. We now know Ronald Alexander can improvise."

Four

Edward was about to take his seat at his desk, when his attention was diverted toward the floor safe next to the wall.

"Harold Lawton was the garment factory manager," Edward said, kneeling and opening up his personal safe. He retrieved a short-barreled revolver. He checked the safety, and slipped it into his left inside coat pocket. He dropped a half dozen extra cartridges into the opposite coat pocket, then slammed the safe closed.

"Naught was done unless he allowed it," Edward continued. "The only person not afraid of Harold Lawton was John Connelly. With the demise of Mister Connelly, the whole world had need to fear Harold Lawton."

"Detective Willoughy," Cadet Brown said, "Your revolver is small. Is it powerful enough?"

Franklin started laughing. "Ye've ne'er seen a BBD actually fire? Wot are they teachin' ya at the academy?"

"It's a point four five oh caliber, short box cattrich, laddie," Lawrence added. "If Willoughby 'ere hits center body mass–and 'e rarely misses–the bullet will likely knock the target off 'is feet."

"Giving me just enough time," Edward said, "to interrogate the man before he expires."

"I'm certain Detective Willoughby will allow you to test fire the weapon sometime, eh Edward?" Patrolman Andreason said. "Now, as to the evidence at hand, we still do not have a murder scene. How's our canvassing going?"

"Half of Southall station is covering the area," Edward said, "augmented by six of our own detectives."

"D'ya think we could lend a hand?" Cadet Peterson said. "It might speed things up."

"We'd probably just get in the way," Edward said. "The search area is somewhat small, and I'm confident the murder scene will be found quickly, once the fog lifts. Let's work the evidence. Add Harold Lawton to our chart, and see how this all fits with the rest of the murders we're investigating."

"Let's process what we *do* know," Lawrence said, "and be ready once the bleedin' necropsies are complete. No pun intended."

The six policemen settled in to the routine of sorting the facts as they currently saw them. Without a workspace large enough, they only created piles. Superintendent McCarthy had guaranteed they would have a secure, permanent place to handle the complexities of the "Cemetery Murders," as the Scotland Yard staff was now calling them.

"Detective Willoughby?" A woman appeared at the corner of his desk.

"I am Willoughby," Edward said.

"Wilimena Lounsberry. Your room is ready, if you'll follow me."

"Cadet Brown, stay with the evidence. The rest of us will follow Miss Lounsberry."

* * * * *

Four floors down, Wilimena used a large key to open a heavy oak door.

"Here you are, gents," she said, pulling hard on the doorknob. The door creaked and the hinges squeaked. "It might not look like much, but it's one of the most secure places in Scotland Yard."

"Thank you Miss Lounsberry," Edward said. "Was this once used for evidence storage?"

"Yes, until we ran out of room," Wilimena said. "It will take some clean up, but you'll have total seclusion. Here's the key. I have the only spare." Miss Lounsberry turned and ascended the stairs.

The room was several times larger than Edward's residence, and offered one color: gray. The wooden storage shelves were painted medium gray, as were the few tables. The walls were a lighter shade of gray, while the floor was smokey gray. Dust was everywhere.

"Well, 'ere's one way to define 'drab'," Franklin said, running his fingers across one of the shelves, then flicking them over the equally dusty floor.

"Perhaps," Edward said, "but it's also neutral."

"Cadet Peterson," Edward said. "Find a broom and some rags. I'll send Cadet Brown to help you clean up."

"Yessir," Peterson said.

"Robert, you and I will go clear out my house, and combine all that evidence into this space."

"Edward," Lawrence said, "I would feel better if we all go to your abode. I'd like to discourage any killers at large."

"Very well," Edward sighed. "Let's move everything from my desk down to this room, and then we can go."

* * * * *

"Only a directive in writing from Superintendent McCarthy or me will get anyone's access to this room." Edward looked at the mountains of evidence on the tables. "Here is the key." He handed the heavy room key to Cadet Peterson. "We should return in a few hours. You and Cadet Brown will clean first, then organize what we have brought from the third floor. We will sort it all upon our return."

"Yessir." The young men began dusting.

* * * * *

Four policemen entered the lobby of Scotland Yard a few moments later and turned toward the street.

"Willoughby," the Desk Sergeant called.

"Yes, Detective Sergeant," Edward replied.

"Someone to see you," he pointed to somewhat scruffy individual sitting on one of the waiting benches.

Lawrence and Franklin reached inside their coat pockets and stepped in front of Edward. Andreason walked toward the man, who had just stood, and kept his head down, assuming a submissive pose. Andreason kept out of the detectives' line of fire.

"I'm Officer Andreason. What business would ye be having with Detective Willoughby this morning, sir?" Robert eyed the man for threatening moves or hidden weapons.

"Carleton Abbey. Abbs is wot they calls me. Wot I 'ave would be personal like, officer," the man replied.

He held a weathered top hat in two shaky hands. His face was dotted with "repairs" to the effects of a dull razor. His clean clothes had seen better times. He wore a threadbare black vest with a white shirt and a frayed silk ascot. A well-worn leather coat covered his torso and protected him from the elements. His tan trousers were ragged at the cuffs and the right shoe sported a hole in the sole.

"I believe the detective to be in danger." He puffed on a meerschaum pipe, sending a cloud of smoke to the ceiling.

"As do we, sir, hence the nervous nature o' the two detectives behind me." Robert motioned for the man to sit on the bench. "We are close associates of Detective Willoughby. Do ye think we could have a chat in a more private place?"

"Would it be possible to git a cup o' tea?"

"I believe we could manage it," Robert grinned. "Now for the serious side of this. You need to allow me to search ye for weapons."

"Absholootley, Officer, er Andereason is it?" Carleton raised his arms.

* * * * *

Carleton Abbey caressed the teacup with both hands as he slurped the brown liquid.

"So Abbs, what is it that brings you all the way from Docklands to Westminster?" Edward asked, as he scrutinized the old man. "I have not heard of you these two years past."

"I've been at Docklands, 'tis true," Carleton took another sip of his tea and closed his eyes, "my that's good, but Sundays I stay at me mum's 'ouse in Kensington. She keeps a bed for me, 'er son and heir.

"I stopped at a pub this night past on the way, and 'ad a few arf an' arfs. Since me mum don't allow no drinkin' or drunks a' 'er place, I plopped down in the bushes in Queens Park, t' sober up a bit before continuin'."

"And what did you see at Queens Park?"

"Two gents, one well-'eeled and one a bit rough-lookin', met near the middle of the park, right near me restin' place. They should a' kept their voices low, considering wot they wuz plannin'.

"Well, the well-heeled feller starts with ya name. 'e pauses, then says 'I want 'im dead.' 'e wants it public and brutal. The sooner the better."

"And what did you do?" Edward looked over at Andreason, who was taking notes.

"Me? Against the likes 'o those two? I stayed right where I wuz. But then a shadow began trailin' the well-off gent. About halfway through the park, this shadow grabbed 'im, using 'is scarf. Once the gent goes limp, the shadow pulls out a razor, and all this blood goes everywhere."

"What did you do then?" Edward was taking furious notes now.

"The shadow left the park, and I went the other direction, careful not to run into either of 'em, the killer or the shadow." Abbs sipped his tea. "As I reached the north gate, I spied a cab, and the cabbie in 'is high perch. The killer comes from the right, and I ducks into the bushes.

"The cabbie jumps down from 'is perch and asks if the killer was ready. 'e said 'e was, and the next word I 'ere is 'I cannot allow you to kill the detective.' I returned to the bushes and waited until the cab left, and I wuz sure the ghost 'ad gone.

"I was plenty sober by then, and I hurried to me mum's, got a bit o' breakfast, then came straight 'ere."

"Why come here at all?" Lawrence asked.

"I owe Detective Willowby, I do." Carleton set down the cup. "Eleven years past, he got me out o' me life o' drinkin' and carryin' on. While I still drinks a bit, I don't carry on no more. Nosiree. I owe detective Edward Willowby for that."

"Abbs, you can still write?" Edward said.

"Another gift ye gave me, sir." Carleton had a twinkle in his eye. "It's because o' that I have me job at Docklands. I'm a dockets-man. I keep track o' things. Yessir, I can surely write."

"Good man," Edward said, patting him on the shoulder. "These gents are going to type up what ya just said, and we're going to ask that ya sign it. Is that alright?"

"Abshootley, Detective Edward Willowby. Abshootley."

"We'll get you a second cup o' tea, too."

"My day's gettin' better all the time." Carleton smiled, revealing yellow and brown teeth, drained the cup, and pushed it across the table at Lawrence.

* * * * *

Franklin trotted to the front desk and shoved a piece of paper toward the desk sergeant. The sergeant read the note and shouted, "Johnnie!" He swiveled to the telegraph operator. "Wire this to Southall Station, straightaway."

"Yes, Sergeant." the young uniformed man snatched the note and jumped back to the telegraph key.

* * * * *

The telegraph operator handed Sergeant Ambrose at Southall Station her latest dispatch:

```
SERGEANTS AMBROSE
AND STEVENSON-STOP-
NEW EVIDENCE JUST
ADMITTED-STOP-
CONCENTRATE SEARCH
FOR CRIME SCENE AT
QUEENS PARK.
```

"Halverson!" Sergeant Ambrose shouted above the din of the station.

"Yes, Sergeant." The uniformed officer pushed his way to the front desk.

"Get this to Sergeant Stevenson, best speed. I believe he's at Kensal Greens Cemetery, main entrance."

"Yes, Sergeant." Halverson grabbed his bicycle and left the station.

"Robison!"

"Yes, Sergeant." A tall officer walked from the hallway.

"Take three officers and scour Queens Park for blood pools. There should be two separate scenes."

"On it." Robison ran down the hallway to the tea room.

"Now if the rain will hold off for another hour or two." Sergeant Ambrose said, looking out the windows at the gray day. He sipped his mug of tea. "Suzanne, wire back to Scotland Yard. We're pursuing this with all haste."

Five

Four officers spread out as they began the search on the south end of Queen's Park, looking for two separate crime scenes.

"Look in the shrubbery, too, lads," one instructed. "We don't want to miss anything."

They proceeded through the park, poking and prodding with their nightsticks. They lifted branches and parted bushes, trying to find something they didn't believe was even there. They were almost halfway through the park.

"Over here," one officer called. "I've got something."

Robison strode to the landscaping in the center of the park. A dark brown stain was unmistakably blood, and there were footprints.

"Good work, Jameson," Robison said. "Mark this area. We'll get help for the rest."

Just then a dozen constables and detectives entered the south side of the park, diverted from the larger search and canvas. Robison explained what they had just found, and now a much larger search team worked the park. Two of the detectives began to process the crime scene. Officer Halverson had the only bicycle, and was sent to Southall Station to send a wire to Edward Willoughby and his team of the development.

Sergeant Stevenson deployed four bobbys to begin his search from the north, and stopped short before they began. The street and sidewalk were covered in blood splatter by the north gate.

"Get one of the detectives, Harold," Stevenson said. "I'll contain this scene. Continue with the search through the park. We know of two murders, but we are not assured those are the only ones. Let's do our due diligence."

"Yes, sergeant," the officers replied, and began the methodical task of checking everything in the immediate area.

* * * * *

Edward and his team began rolling carts laden with evidence through the lobby of Scotland Yard when his name was called out.

"Willoughby," the desk sergeant said. "I've two wires for you from Southall Station. Seems you were right." The smiling sergeant handed both dispatches to Edward.

The first wire read:
```
FOUND ONE BLOOD
POOL AT QUEENS
PARK—STOP—
CONTINUING THE
SEARCH.
```

The second wire followed the first:
```
FOUND THE SECOND
BLOOD POOL AT
QUEENS PARK—STOP—
SEARCH COMPLETE—
STOP—COME AT YOUR
EARLIEST
CONVENIENCE.
```

"Thank you." Edward said. "Is Abbs still here?"

"Aye, he is indeed," the sergeant sighed. "I fear he is depleting our supply of Earl Grey."

"And worth every penny, sergeant." He looked at his team and the carts. "I'll be with him shortly."

"I'll get you some people to help with your collection," the Sergeant said. "Go. Take care of this most important witness."

"Thank you." Edward walked to his team and the evidence. He handed the wire memos to Andreason. "I'll go thank Abbs for his help, and rescue our tea supply. I'll see that he gets back to his mum's."

"We'll be fine. Take care of Abbs." Robert smiled as he read the memos and passed them to Lawrence and Franklin.

* * * * *

"Abbs," Edward said, entering the coffee and tearoom. "Your information has proved to be accurate. Thank you. But, it is time for you to be off to visit with your mum."

"Are ye certain? I could stay a while, per'aps even be of some 'elp."

"Please visit with your mum," Edward said. "You will not have her forever, you know."

"Alright, detective." He gulped the last of the tea in his cup. "Most of the day is gone, though."

"Which is why I have retained the services of Charlie the cabbie. He is waiting outside, and I have already paid him. Oh, because you were so helpful, here is one pound for you."

Edward pressed the coin into the old man's weathered hand.

"Ye have always been good to me. Thank ye." Abbs was near tears.

"Get out of here before we are both blubbering fools."

With that, Abbs was out of Scotland Yard like fog in the wind.

* * * * *

"What d'ya think, Edward?" Robert studied the blood in the shrubs at Queens Park.

"This would be Harold Lawton's blood." Edward looked every direction. "He would be walking back to his own carriage. Wilford Davis would take a wide route to his ride, to ensure he was not being followed.

"The scarf would make the perfect strangle tool. Thirty seconds, give or take, and he would be dead, or close to it. The slicing was the signature, to make sure he had expired."

"What about Wilford Davis?" Franklin said. "He would have been on guard."

"Perhaps," Edward said, "but would he suspect a cabbie to be dangerous?"

"Careless," Lawrence breathed. "One flippant moment, and your life is forfeit."

"Precisely," Edward said.

"So, Wilford exits the East Gate, and Ronald Alexander – if this is really his work – exits the West Gate, beating the cautious killer for hire to the cab."

"So, is Ronald Alexander really a cabbie, or did he steal the cab?" Cadet Brown said. "He would also have to steal the clothes."

"Unless he killed the cabbie and took his belongings," Cadet Peterson added.

"We should be looking for any stolen cabs or missing cabbies," Edward said. "Sergeant Stevenson, did either of those occur during the night?"

"Not at our station," Stevenson said. "At least, not until I began assisting you all this morning. Sergeant Ambrose might have an update, though."

"Wilford Davis lives in Paddington, not Kensington," Lawrence said. "We should get Paddington station involved there. We can wire them from Southall. With your permission, Sergeant Stevenson?"

"Absolutely, detective," the sergeant said.

"Lawrence," Edward said, "you and Franklin go to Paddington. Robert and I will inform Harold Lawton's next of kin."

Six

Battersea Park:

Edward double-checked the address and scratched his head. The cab stopped at 847 Warrington Gardens, just south of Battersea Park. The working class neighborhood seemed to be an out of place for someone in senior management of a large company.

Edward Willoughby and Robert Andreason opened their umbrellas and stepped into the midday air, just as the rain let up a bit. Edward paid and thanked the cabbie, then looked at the bright red door. He rapped the heavy brass knocker three times, then waited.

The door opened slowly, and a teary-eyed woman with a handkerchief in one hand looked at the two officers. "Since you're the police, I assume yer not bringin' me good news," the woman sighed. "Don't just stand out there in the rain, come on in." She pushed the door open and walked into her parlor.

"You are Harriet Lawton, are you not?" Edward said.

"While, ye may meet a thousan' people a year, Detective Willoughby," the gray-haired woman quipped, "I don't. I remember ye from me husband's trial, and your insistence that he is some sort of common criminal. Yes, I am Harriet Lawton."

* * * * *

"23 Gloucester Mews, sirs," the cabbie said.

"Thank you, sir," Franklin said, paying the driver.

"Stay dry." the cabbie slapped the reins on the back of his horse, and was soon gone.

The blue-gray door had no knocker, so Lawrence removed his glove and rapped on the wood. A rattling could be heard inside, yet no one made an effort to open the door. Lawrence knocked a second time.

"Police," he said. "Open the door please."

"*Please* ya say?" the voice of an old woman boomed through the heavy oak door. "The coppers I know would ne'er say *please*."

"We're not ordinary coppers, ma'am," Lawrence said. "We're from Scotland Yard."

Before they could say anything, the door opened wide. A woman, standing no more than four feet, waved them inside.

"Anything for the police," she said. "Yesserie, I want to keep on the good side of every copper I can. Especially those fellas from Scotland Yard. Make yerselves at home. Tea?"

"Yes ma'am, that would be lovely," Lawrence said.

A few minutes later, the woman placed a porcelain tea set on a low table in her parlor. Each officer took a cup and thanked her.

"Sugar anyone?" She set the bowl on the tray, took a cup and settled onto a French Provincial chair. "Now, what would Scotland Yard be wanting with me?"

"Actually, it's Wilford Davis who concerns us," Franklin said.

"I see." She sipped some tea and continued. "So, what has Wilford been up to?"

"How are you related to Mister Davis?" Franklin said.

"He's me boy, me offspring."

"And your name would be?"

"Ovella. Ovella Davis."

"Missus Davis…"

"Miss," she interrupted. "Mister Davis ran out on me and Wilford more than thirty years ago. I ain't seen 'im since he disappeared."

"Miss Davis, when was the last time you saw your son?"

"This Wednesday last," she said. "He was meeting a business associate."

"And what kind of business is your son in?"

"He don't talk about work at home. I only know he provides for the both of us." She studied the two officer's faces. "Wot's this all about?"

"I'm afraid I have some bad news, Miss Davis," Franklin said. "Your son was the victim of foul play this night last."

"How foul?" Her hard eyes began to soften. She set her teacup down.

"He was murdered."

"Murdered? Murdered!" She looked down at her hands, then the tears began to flow. "Well, don't just sit there drinkin' up all me tea. Go out and catch the bastard who killed 'im."

"We have more than twenty officers doing just that, ma'am." Lawrence said. "It falls to us to inform the next of kin. I suppose that would be you, Miss Davis?"

"I suppose it would. I suppose it would." Ovella looked around the cozy flat. She stopped short of looking all the way around the room and said, "So, where is me son's body?"

"At Scotland Yard."

"I can identify 'im if ya need me to."

"No need, Miss Davis," Lawrence said. "Your son and I had an encounter several years past, and I already identified him."

"An encounter, eh?" Ovella smirked. "Since my Wilford didn't end up in the slammer, I suppose ye ne'er convicted 'im?"

"That would be correct, Miss Davis. And since he has expired, I never will. Convict 'im, that is."

"Miss Davis," Franklin said, "Is that your son?" pointing to a framed photograph on the mantel.

"It is indeed," Ovella said.

"Do ye know who is wi' 'im?"

"No, but 'e was awful proud o' that picture."

"Might we borrow it? It may help with the investigation. You'll get it back."

"As long as I get it back, yer welcome to it."

"And if we might," Lawrence said, "could we see 'is room?"

The room was bare, nearly Spartan. The bed was a bit on the small side, with plain white sheets and a gray wool blanket. It was topped with a flat goose down pillow.

There were no wall adornments. Franklin opened a small desk drawer, only to find a dozen sheets of blank paper and a lead pencil.

"He spent one night in three 'ere the past few years," Ovella said. "I 'ave no idea where he spent the rest of the time."

"Where was he employed?" Lawrence said.

"He never said." The woman drew a ragged breath. "He only said he was into contract work."

"He had no office? No place he would go each day?"

"Not that he said."

"Did he drink? Was there a pub he frequented?"

* * * * *

"Missus Lawton, this is some fine tea," Edward said, setting down his cup. He waited for the mature woman to make the inquiry. He had done far too many Next-of-Kin notifications to provide the information too early.

"I have a question," Edward continued, "Mister Lawton is a very well-paid manager in the garment industry. You can easily afford a larger home in a more prestigious neighborhood. Why stay here in Battersea Park?"

"And be all uppity like my husbands' associates?" Harriet set the teacup on its saucer. "No sir. I was born in Battersea, and that's where I aim to breathe my last. Now what terrible news do you have for me?"

"I'm afraid your husband has been murdered. You have my condolences."

Harriet Lawton set her cup and saucer on the serving tray, folded her hands and took in a long breath. "You're certain?" Her eyes searched Edward's.

"Yes, ma'am." Edward locked eyes with her. "I made the identification myself. You can be spared a visit to the morgue." He paused some moments. "Is there someone we can get for you? A neighbor, perhaps?"

"Missus Oglethorpe, that's Maggie Oglethorpe, next door, at eight forty nine. But you'll be wanting to look through my husband's things, won't ya?"

"Yes, ma'am, we will." Edward finished his tea, and set the cup on the tray. "Officer Andreason, would you fetch Missus Oglethorpe, while I begin the search?"

"Very good, sir." Robert grabbed his hat and stepped toward the door.

"Shall we, detective?" Harriet held her hands out to indicate the entire house was available to the detective.

Edward and Robert searched every room in the house, which revealed little. Harrold kept his work away from his residence, concentrating instead on his family. Photographs of a son and a daughter figured prominently in every corner of the house.

"Missus Lawton," Edward said, standing in the doorway of the kitchen. I believe we are finished. You have my sincere condolences."

"Thank you, Detective," Harriet said. "I'll walk you out."

Edward noticed a photograph above the mantel in the parlor. He studied it for a moment, noting the faces in a country setting. Robert looked over his shoulder. Edward shook his head, a signal to keep quiet.

"Missus Lawton," Edward said, "what is the nature of this photograph?"

"Oh, that thing," she replied. "Each year the lads from work go up to Oxfordshire for a week of golfin' and drinkin'. I think it's more for drinkin' than anythin' else."

"Would it be alright to take it with us? It might be helpful."

"Certainly," she said. "If yer going to take it, please leave the frame."

"Thank you, madam." Edward turned the frame over and removed the photograph, placing the empty frame on the mantel. The two detectives tipped their hats and let themselves outside, into the morning rain.

"I hate these notifications," Robert said. "I never get used to them."

"Pray that you never will, Robert," was all Edward said. "Now we need to go to Harold Lawton's office."

Seven

Limehouse, London, 24 Norway Place. Not the location Edward had imagined a wealthy manager of a large manufacturer would have his office, but stranger things had happened during this investigation. The graystone building definitely contained offices, and business could easily be conducted there. But it was two or three quality steps lower than it need be.

The location did place the office close to both docks and the garment factories. This would assist in the amelioration of any issues arising from both the delivery of supplies and the actual production of the garments.

Edward and Robert opened the front door of the office and stepped in. The lobby contained a single desk and a secretary. Behind the desk was a door. The rest of the room was plain, nearly devoid of decor. An attractive middle-aged woman looked up from her typing.

"Detective Edward Willoughby," she said, "good morning to ya."

"Margaret," Edward said, "good to see you again. How goes it?"

"Could be better, could be worse. Still single, I see. When you going to get around to courtin' me?"

"Some time after you, too, are single, dear lady."

"Spoilsport. Who do you have wi' you today?"

"Patrolman Robert Andreason, madam." Robert stuck out his hand.

"Nice to meet you, Patrolman Robert Andreason," Margaret said. "And you dispense with the formalities. It's just Margaret."

"Then it's a pleasure to meet you Margaret." The two shook hands.

"Edward," Margaret said, "if you're here to see Mister Lawton, 'e's not in yet."

"Actually, we have both seen Harold Lawton today," Edward said. "I'm afraid I have some bad news. Harold met with foul play this night past."

"No!" Margaret looked down at her desk. "You're certain?"

"Yes. I made the verification myself. I'm sorry, Margaret."

"Sometimes the invincible fall," Margaret said.

"Beg you pardon?"

"Oh, it's just that Harold would regularly imply he was invincible." Margaret paused. "I suppose that's not true, is it?"

"No, it isn't. I need to see Harold's desk, to see if there is anything of value. Anything which will aid in solving the crime."

"Well," Margaret said, straightening her dress and sitting up in her chair, "you know you need a warrant."

Edward reached inside his brief case and retrieved a document. "I came prepared."

She took her time reading the document, and after a while looked up at Edward. "It appears to be in order. Come, let me show you 'is desk." She stood and opened the door behind her. They entered to a sea of desks, where several dozen women worked in silence.

Several made ledger entries, a few typed documents, while others verified manifests and invoices.

Margaret marched through the din to the back wall. A carved oak door guarded the entrance to the office of Harold Lawton, and she inserted a key into the brass lock. *Click!*

She pushed the heavy panel open, and switched on the lights. A Persian rug covered the floor and a teak executive's desk dominated the space. A half dozen Impressionist paintings hung from the walls, and file drawers lined one end of the room.

"Here are the keys, Edward," Margaret said, and handed a large key ring to the detective. "Lock up when you're done."

"Thank you, we will," Edward said. Margaret winked and closed the door behind her.

"Where do ye want to start, Edward?" Robert said, looking at all the potential hiding places.

"I'll begin with his desk and calendar, and you can peruse his files. That should keep us out of each other's way."

Files were scrutinized, the desk all but taken apart, and during the next four hours Edward and Robert made a shambles of the opulent business room. Edward moved over to the file cabinets once everything in the desk had been examined, giving Robert a much-needed hand.

Hundreds of files in a seeming nonsensical order stared at them. These were the organizational tools of running a garment factory, not a criminal organization.

The hours rolled by, and nothing revealed itself. Every file had been reviewed, and everything appeared to be in order. The office was now filled with stacks and stacks of files, set in the specific order they were removed.

Something shouted out to Edward. He just could not place his finger on it. Nothing the least bit secret had been disovered. After a hundred investigations, even tiny secrets were kept in file folders, yet here there was naught.

He sat in the large swivel desk chair and stared at nothing in particular. He raised his head slightly.

"See something, Edward?" Robert said.

"It's not in the files. It's in the cabinets themselves."

"Oh?"

"Look at them. Aren't the bases overly-tall?"

"I just thought that to be the style of the furniture."

"As did I." Edward walked to the nearest cabinet. "See this dent here? If I kick the wood at that same spot…" he lightly kicked the oak fascia with his shoe. A drawer popped forward.

Two heads stared at the contents. Stacks of money, British pounds, German Deutch Marks, American Dollars, and Argentine Pesos filled a good portion of the space. Beneath the money were a dozen file folders, and a canvas shoulder bag. On top of all of it was a revolver.

"Harold did not trust anyone, I suppose," Edward said.

"This must have been his travel money," Robert added. "Hullo. Are those passports?"

"Yes," Edward said. "In the file labeled 'bug out'. The remaining files must contain incriminating evidence on someone, which might give Mr. Lawton a clear path to leave the British Empire."

"Do you think the rest of these people have similar packages?"

"Time will tell. I doubt we could get a search warrant, based upon this discovery."

They took the next hour to put all the files back into the drawers. They emptied the secret drawer into the canvas bag, and bid farewell to Margaret on the way out of the office.

Eight

"What did you find out?" Edward said to Lawrence and Franklin as they arrived in the basement at Scotland Yard.

"Only a photograph, I'm afraid," Franklin said, handing the photo to Edward.

"Like this one?" Edward laid Harriet Lawton's photograph on his desk.

"Lord Lumme," Lawrence. "I'll bet there are more of these out there, somewhere. A connection, perhaps?"

"Well, there's Langley Smythe and Harley Winthorpe." Edward pointed.

"Two of the garment seven," Cadet Peterson said.

"And Wilford Davis, in better times, and Harold Lawton," Robert said. "The rest are unknown to me. Does anyone recognize them?"

No? Then let's look at the photograph in a different way. Instead of 'who', perhaps we should look at 'where' the photograph is from. This is an estate, is it not?"

"Yes, but it's all lawn," Lawrence studied the grounds.

"Look closer gentlemen," Edward said. "The upper right corner. A structure."

The back of the photograph said, "Wantage, Oxfordshire, 1889." The photograph out of the frame revealed a larger portion of a stone building, possibly an estate.

"The windows are Georgian," Cadet Peterson said. "Possibly newer construction, from the looks."

"How can you be so certain, cadet?" Franklin said.

"Oh, Cadet Peterson fancies himself as a purveyor of architecture," Cadet Brown said.

"Notwithstanding," Edward said, "this is a very large estate. Not many of these exist in Oxfordshire, or anywhere else for that matter. Peterson, you identified the style of architecture, now search the county records for the largest, most expensive estates in the area. Once found, search for the owners and make a connection to Wilford Davis, or the members of the Garment Seven."

"Come on, laddie," Franklin said, reaching for his hat. "I wuz plying through those records this year last. I can at least get ye pointed in the right direction. We begin with the Domesday Book, which lists all property in England."

"It's getting late everyone," Edward said, looking at the wall clock. "Let's continue this in the morning. We will begin the canvas from the Ovella Davis residence, and find out where Wilford spent two-thirds of his time. Cadet Brown, there is still a lot of organization to do."

"Understood," Cadet Brown said. "I should be able to get this done by the day's end tomorrow."

"Very good. We'll be off then." Edward handed Franklin the key to the room. "Get the two cadets started in the morning, and we will be back as soon as we complete our canvas."

Nine

The fog was so thick that the shops had lights at noon. There were few people in the street, making the canvas more difficult. Lawrence and Edward pulled their collars up and tightened their scarves about their necks, yet the cold still knifed its way through to their skin.

"We'll have precious little time, Edward," Lawrence said. "The day-light only begins from nine in the morning, and immediately after four it'll be gone. This may take several days."

"Aye," Edward said. "Unfortunately, it takes as long as it takes. Perhaps tomorrow Franklin and both cadets will aid us with our search."

The light was an opaque, dingy yellow. Torches were used as guides to carriages at mid-day, but gave scarcely any light through the fog. The three officers completed a circle search of a half mile from the Davis residence before the failing light caused them to stop at the Elephant and Castle, a somewhat large pub.

"Ah, do ye smell it Edward?" Robert said. "Alcohol-soaked oak. There's no other odor on the planet quite like it which welcomes a stranger."

They all removed their coats, scarves and hats and sat at a booth near the back of the establishment. Their notebooks dominated the table as they reviewed them.

The barkeep approached. He was old, his burgundy-colored cheeks wrinkled from years somewhere else, perhaps weathered as a seaman. He was drying his hands on a towel.

The man eyed the three men with great care. "What can I get for London's finest?"

"Are we that obvious?" Edward said.

"Hell no," he responded. "Officer Lawrence Griffin and I 'ave 'ad dealins over the years, 'aven't we?"

"Paul," Lawrence stuck out his hand, and Paul shook it vigorously. "It's been wot, four years?"

"Five. But I'm not countin'," he winked.

"Well, Paul," Edward said, "how's about a pint o' yer favorite brew fer all three of us?"

"Edward. Edward Willoughby." Edward shook hands with Paul. "And this other gent is Robert Andreason. We're on duty more often than not, but we have had a rough day, and a pint will help us forget it."

"Comin' right up." Paul wandered back to the bar.

Paul returned with the three beers, and looked at Lawrence. "Lookin' for somethin'?"

"Actually, yes," Lawrence said. "Do ye know of Wilford Davis?"

"Tall gent, small scar on 'is left cheek?"

"Yes, that'd be 'im."

"He stays sometimes wi' 'is mum over on Gloucester Mews, if I recall. He pops in from time to time. Quiet man. Tips Constance, me barmaid, well."

"When 'e ain't stayin' wi' 'is mum, do ye know where 'e might flop?"

"I know 'e takes the train to Kings Cross, 'cause 'e asked about the fare."

"Thanks." Edward sipped the beer. "My, ain't that good. Great choice, Paul. What else can ye tell us about 'im?"

"Well, he's not a bloke I'd invite 'ome wi' me. Nosirree, 'e just looks dangerous, you know wot I mean?"

"I believe we do. Thanks again, Paul." The barkeep wiped down two tables on his way back to the bar.

"Ten minutes, and we've accomplished more than our combined efforts of a whole day. We need to frequent more pubs," Robert said, raising his glass. "Here's to good, solid neighborhood establishments."

"Here, here," Lawrence and Edward said together.

* * * *

The next morning the fog was replaced by a heavy drizzle, necessitating umbrellas by all six officers. Sketches had been produced of Wilford Davis and all of the Garment Seven. They stepped out of Kings Cross Station and stopped beneath the arched opening of the building. Two other detectives had joined them, so they could cover four directions in teams of two.

"Remember everyone, we canvas until twelve o'clock, then return to the station here." He nodded to all the officers, and said "Officer Andreason and I will go north. The rest of you have your directions. Let's see what we can find in four hours."

Eight o'clock was pre-dawn, but the streets were already busy with people going to work. It was too early for shoppers, and the working class was focused on getting to their places of employment. No one wanted to be delayed, even if it was to talk to a policeman.

The search was slow at best. The officers made their way out, covering as much of Kings Cross as possible. Franklin and Cadet Peterson, covering the south of the station, were just about to turn back when they noticed an upstairs office sign: "W. Davis, Investigations".

The two mounted the stairs and turned down the hallway to the office. The door was ajar. Splinters from the doorframe littered the floor. Franklin pulled out his revolver and pushed the door open. Papers littered the office, desk drawers were askew. The wall safe was exposed, but not open.

No one else was in the room.

"Get back to Kings Cross Station," Franklin said. "Bring everyone here, best speed."

"You'll be safe here?" Peterson's eyes were wide open.

"I'll be fine," he said, patting his gun. "Go."

* * * * *

The six officers and two cadets began cleaning up the office, stacking the papers on the desk and trying to make sense of the "Detective" Wilford Davis. They were almost half finished, when there were steps at the door.

"Did someone call for an officer?" A uniformed bobby asked.

"Yes we did," Edward said, straightening his tie. "Officer…"

"Duckworth, sir, Howard Duckworth. And you would be?"

"Detective Edward Willoughby, Scotland Yard," Edward said, showing his credentials. "These other gents are associates, either directly from Scotland Yard, or attached to it.

"We're investigating Wilford Davis, who conducts private investigations from this office."

"Beggin' yer pardon, sir," the Bobby said, "but if Wilford Davis is a private investigator, then I'm a pirate on the Spanish Main."

"Then the sign in the window is misleading?"

"Without question," Officer Duckworth said. "The man sits behind that desk there, day after day, doing little except drinkin' tea and watchin' the street. I'm not certain how the man earns his keep, but I don't believe it to be honest in nature."

"D'ye ever see 'im leave the premises?" Lawrence asked.

"Only for lunch at the Blarney Stone, across the way." Duckworth looked at the mess of papers in the office and said, "So, what has Wilford Davis done to earn the attention of Scotland Yard?"

"He's gotten himself dead," Edward announced.

"Dead? When?"

"Two nights past. Did you notice anyone coming or going, who might be responsible for the rummaging of this office?"

"No, detective, though I was aware Mr. Davis had not been in for two days."

"Would that be unusual?"

"Not really. A few days each week he does not come in to the office. I figured he was bored, and needed a break." The officer touched his chin. "Say, 'ow did Mr. Davis die?"

"He was murdered. But 'twas not in your jurisdiction."

"That does not surprise me." The officer looked around the room, with its scattered papers and overturned furniture. "Wot is it ye need from me?"

"Security, Officer Duckworth. We need to ensure no one else disturbs this area until we've 'ad time to process the evidence."

"Allow me a half hour to check in with me sergeant, sir, and Kings Cross Station will be 'appy to assist ye."

Ten

Officer Duckworth returned with his sergeant less than a half hour later. The sergeant was ramrod straight and clean-shaven. His hair was neatly trimmed and his uniform impeccable.

"Ah, you have returned," Edward said. "Sergeant, I am Detective Edward Willoughby, Scotland Yard."

"Sergeant Owens," he said, removing his glove to shake hands with Edward. "I understand Mister Davis has met with foul play, two nights past."

"Indeed," Edward said. "In Queen's Park."

"How did ye end up here? It's a far piece from Queens Park to Kings Cross."

"We spent yesterday and part of today canvassing, attempting to ascertain 'ow he spent his time. A Paddington barkeep pointed us toward Kings Cross, and 'ere we are."

"D'ya think he conducted his killing for hire out of this office?" Sergeant Owens scanned the interior of the room.

"Too soon to tell." Edward said. "We'll have to go through all this paper, and we're waiting on a warrant to open the safe, and any hidden compartments we might find."

"The warrant would be from magistrate Brumley?" The sergeant continued to observe the office.

"Exactly," Lawrence said.

"He takes his midday meal at the Blarney Stone, across the street. He's probably there right now."

"You don't say," Edward said. "If your man could secure the premises, we could stand to have a bite ourselves."

"He can indeed," Sergeant Owens said.

"Sergeant, d'ya care to join us?"

"I don't mind if I do. Officer Duckworth, please secure the premises. No one has access, save Detective Willoughby's men."

"Very good, sergeant." Duckworth stood at attention by the door.

"I'm proceeding at a good pace here," Cadet Peterson said. "Could ya bring me back a san'wich?"

"Me too," Cadet Brown added. "We should have most of this organized by the time you return."

"Very well," Edward said. "Just compile the papers. No searching, not without the warrant."

"Yessir," they both said as one.

* * * * *

The Blarney Stone was a small pub, capable of handling a bit more than a dozen patrons at once. Three tables occupied the center of the room, and a few stools decorated the bar itself. There was a secondary counter facing the street with four stools. The whole musty affair smelled inviting.

In the far corner sat a well-dressed man eating a stew. His hand clutched a pint of lager.

"Sergeant Owens," the man said, "Wot brings ye 'ere so early in the day?"

"Scotland Yard, regarding Wilford Davis."

"Ya don't say?" He looked at Edward. "That'd be you, sir?"

"Detective Edward Willoughby, at your service."

"Ah, so it was you who requested access to Wilford Davis's office, and wall safe?"

"Yessir."

"And where might Mister Davis be?"

"In the Scotland Yard Morgue, sir," Edward said. "He's been murdered."

"You're certain it was murder?"

"His throat was slit."

"Ah. In that case, I'll sign your warrant right now." Brumley retrieved a folded document from his right inside coat pocket and a fountain pen from his left. He carefully unscrewed the cap, unfolded the paper, and signed the bottom of the document.

"There, Detective, all set. Would ye be having a meal, as well?"

"Sergeant Owens highly recommends this place," Edward said, smiling, "so we have no choice but to be patrons."

"Well then, me boys, pull up extra tables and chairs and let's get to it." Brumley looked up at the bar. "Olsen, kind sir. Looks like London's Finest are going to grace your establishment for lunch."

* * * * *

Peterson and Brown worked the papers with a speed Officer Duckworth did not think was possible. They said few words like "Brown?" or "Wallace?" or "November?" and a new paper was placed neatly on a stack of seemingly incoherent paper. Once all the paper was on the proper stack, they continued organizing. The appropriate file folder was located, and the paper was inserted and placed in the appropriate drawer of the tall filing cabinet.

The last paper was re-filed just before Edward and the rest of the men returned from lunch. A paper sack held sandwiches for the two cadets.

* * * * *

Edward stood in the doorway and just stared. The room looked like an office once more, and not an area of destruction. The chairs and desks were upright and every piece of paper was filed. Even the desk pens and pencils were in place.

"You've earned a well-deserved break." Edward set the sandwiches on the desk. "Relax and enjoy your repast."

"Thank you sir," Peterson said He sipped from an ornate teacup.

"And we have a signed warrant," Franklin said. "The locksmith should be along soon.

"So, wot 'ave ye learned laddies?" Lawrence said.

"He was…" Cadet Peterson wiped his mouth. "He was very well organized. The problem is that what we are seeing only look like transactions for investigative services. Sorry sir, it was hard to organize the paper without reading it, at least a little."

"Understood," Edward said, and took a deep breath. "Very well. What do you have?"

"Reginald Naughton has a very thick file. As a member of the Garment Seven, he is suspect. I just don't know how." Cadet Peterson scrunched his forehead.

"John Connelly's file is not so thick as Mr. Naughton's," Cadet Brown added, "but it's close. These two individuals kept Wilford Davis busy."

"But who is Janet Naughton?" Cadet Peterson asked.

"Another member of the Garment Seven," Edward said. "A sadistic bitch, pardon my language, who kept the workers in line. The disciplinarian. What else do you have?"

"Harold Lawton is a recent addition," Cadet Brown said. "First entry is three days ago."

"Let me see that file."

"He's not yet in a file. He's only in the ledger."

They laid the large green book on the desk and opened it up.

Wilford Detective Services
1892
Records and Services

"It's on page seven, sir."

$\mathcal{D}$ate	$\mathcal{C}$lient	$\mathcal{S}$ervice	$\mathcal{A}$mount
1892/20/3	Livingston, Laura	S&R	£20
1892/21/3	Smith, David	M&L	£50
1892/22/3	Lawton, Harold	D&D	£5000/£5000

"What in the devil does D&D mean?" Lawrence said.

"Death and Deliver?" Cadet Brown said.

"Perhaps," Edward said. "Perhaps not. At any rate, not cheap. Half down, half upon delivery. Did we find any cash on Mr. Davis?"

"We didn't look that far," Franklin said, "especially since I recognized the bugger. There was no need to check 'is pockets."

"We'll check with the coroner upon our return to The Yard," Edward said.

Heavy feet arrived at the top of the stairs.

"Morton Wallace. Who called for a locksmith?" a short, stooped man in his fifties said. He was wearing a neat pair of coveralls, and carried a heavy tool bag.

"That'd be us," Lawrence showing him his police identification.

"Very well." He stepped into the room and pointed to the wall safe. "Is that it?"

"Yes. It's all yours," Edward said. "How long to get inside?"

"No time at all, providing you all keep out o' me way."

* * * * *

The locksmith worked steadily and slowly. The speed, or lack of it, grated on the policemen's nerves. Fifteen minutes passed, and Morton rotated the handle on the safe. The locksmith started to open the door when Edward stopped him.

"I'd re-think that move if I were you." Edward pointed to the top inside of the door, where a wire was attached. "I have seen this before. To protect their secrets, criminals set explosives or acid inside safes such as this." He reached inside and unhooked both ends of the wire. He ran his fingers around the inside of the door, and found no more traps.

"Now you may open it, sir," Edward said.

"No sir," he said. "I'll leave that honor to you." The locksmith backed away from the steel door.

"Very well." Edward pulled the door open to reveal several sticks of dynamite. And hundreds of records. There were weapons. A shotgun, three rifles, a dozen handguns. And money.

"Look at all that cash," Cadet Brown said. "I could make a living on that small pile over there. So, why did he keep on killin'?"

"Everybody has to have something to occupy their time," Edward said. "And perhaps he liked it."

"Liked it?" Cadet Peterson said. "How can he like it?"

"We've all seen worse, laddie," Franklin said. "When it's just you and your craft, that's all that matters."

Eleven

The wagon arrived late in the afternoon, and the sun had set. It was complete with four armed officers. The transfer of the weapons, cash, and documents was finished after dusk, and Willoughby's concerned look said a lot.

"Sergeant Owens, you've been a great help," Edward said. "Now that everything has been removed from Wilford Davis' office, a police seal will be sufficient. A guard should be unnecessary."

"I'll have the local patrolman swing by daily, to ensure the seal is unbroken," Sergeant Owens said. "I'll do that until probate clears."

"Thank you, sergeant." Edward looked at his team. "Very well. Lawrence, you and Franklin are inside the wagon with me. Officer Andreason, make sure our two cadets get home. We'll store all this evidence at The Yard tonight. We'll resume our evidence collection in the morning."

"Very good Edward," Robert responded. "Keep a sharp eye. I don't trust the darkness." He looked about him.

"We will," Lawrence answered, who closed and locked the door from the inside.

Two armed policemen rode atop the wagon, and four more on horseback.

"Let's just hope this show of force keeps the street urchins away," Franklin said.

"And perhaps we're ahead of anyone serious enough to confront us." Edward had his Bulldog in his lap. The two detectives brandished their pistols as well. The half hour ride was fraught with tension. Every turn, every bump signaled the end of the world for the policemen. Men would appear out of the dense fog, and disappear with a speed that left everyone in the caravan wondering if anyone was even there.

Gas lamps cast an eerie glow and menacing shadows everywhere. Phantoms appeared and disappeared with more speed than the passing people. Several times during the journey, the men atop the wagon trained their weapons at naught but a shadow.

Final turn. The iron gates opened and a dozen guards greeted the wagon and its cargo. Nothing had happened, and the policemen and the evidence arrived safely inside Scotland Yard.

They exited the wagon to see a much relieved Superintendent McCarthy standing with the additional officers to assist getting the trove of evidence into the bowels of the building.

"Willoughby," the Superintendent said, "well done. Well done indeed."

"The credit for the find goes to Detective McTavish and Cadet Brown," Edward said. "'Twas they who found the office. Good, solid police work."

"Congratulations, Detective McTavish," He said. "Where might Cadet Brown be?"

"The lad was exhausted, sir," Franklin said. "Officer Andreason is escorting our two young prodigies home for the evening. They'll be back first thing in the morning."

"Very good," he shook Franklin's hand. "I'll pop by in the morning to congratulate the young man."

"Thank you sir, he'd appreciate it."

"In the meantime," Edward said, "let's get this evidence into a secure location."

The officers jumped to the task, and in less than a half hour everything from Wilford Davis' office was secure in the new task force center in the basement of Scotland Yard.

The cash was placed in the walk-in vault on the ground floor of the building. The vault had two security guards for around-the-clock protection. The heavy door slammed shut, and the officers assumed their sentry positions. The senior accountant turned toward Detective Willoughby with his ledger.

"563,483 Pounds Sterling." He looked over his spectacles. "Is that what you thought sir?"

"We rough-estimated 563," Edward said. "I'm glad we were reasonably close."

"Humpf," said the account, who closed his ledger and walked down the hall.

"Humourless gent," Edward said.

"Satisfied, Edward?" Lawrence said.

"Now I am." Edward took one final look, and turned toward the door. Lawrence and Franklin flanked him as they walked to the lobby, and Charlie the cabbie.

* * * * *

Edward closed the door behind him and took off his scarf and coat. The shoes were next, and he put on his rabbit fur-lined slippers. He was starving, but he doubted that he had anything worth eating so late.

He heated some water and poured some lapsang souchong tea leaves into the teapot. That smoky taste would surely wake him up. He cut up some of Mrs. Whitehead's homemade bread and spread fresh butter on the slices. He savoured the blend of flavours as he poured the water over the tea leaves. Now he might be able to relax.

Now for my pipe, Edward thought. He packed and tamped the Nottingham tobacco into the bowl, lit the leaves and puffed on the vulcanite stem connected to the aged briarwood bowl, now glowing red. He tossed the spent match into the fireplace.

Edward closed his eyes and thought about Valeriya Kipriyanov, the tall Russian goddess. *Such pleasures are allowed this late at night.* He luxuriated for a half hour.

He sipped the tea, puffed on the pipe, and munched on the bread as he summed up the day.

Oh well, he sighed, *back to work. A profitable venture all round,* he thought. He re-read his notes a half dozen times before heading toward his bedroom. Sleep overtook him sometime after midnight. His snoring drifted out onto the street.

* * * * *

A shadow left its hiding place across the street from Edward Willoughby's Kensington flat and floated away into the fog, its protection no longer needed. A cabbie headed back to Paddington, to home and a good night's sleep.

Twelve

Darkness still covered the neighborhood when Edward's clock shocked him awake. "Why did Auntie have such a loud alarm?" His shaking hand turned the damned thing off.

Five o'clock.

Heavy cotton robe on, slippers on, and the flat felt so cold. Edward trotted to the fireplace, to find there were no leftover embers from the previous night. *Damn.* He prepared the tender, kindle, and three logs to light and rubbed his hands to warm them up, so he could strike a match to get the fire going.

The small flame warmed his hands enough to go to the kitchen and set a pot of water for tea. Edward walked back to the small fire to warm himself while the water heated.

He was so engrossed with the flame that he forgot about the teapot. The hissing whistle snapped him back to the present and he snatched the "whistler" from the spout. He poured the water, and waited. Not a dark enough brown to be proper tea, but progress was being made.

He sat in his chair in front of the fire with a hot cup of not-ready tea.

Now if I can only get warm.

Edward began to ponder the case.

* * * * *

"Good morning, Detective Sergeant Johnson." A cheery Detective Willoughby said as he bounced into Scotland Yard.

"Sleep well, did ya?" the aging man behind the podium said.

"I did indeed," Edward said.

"Well, I have nothing for ya, if that's wot yer after."

"Not at all, detective sergeant, not at all," Edward said. "We have plenty to keep us busy for a few days."

"I heard ye made quite a haul in Kings Cross."

"Lots to process. Much to compile."

"Well quit yer gloating and get to it."

"I'm off." Edward saluted, spun on his heels and trotted toward the stairs. Detective Sergeant Johnson smirked, took a sip of his tea, and went back to his daily routine.

* * * * *

Cadets Brown and Peterson were already hard at work, moving piles of recently disorganized documents.

"Do they even understand the concept of organization?" Peterson said.

"I think not," Brown answered. "But in their defense, they were concerned about getting all this to a secure area."

"How do we prevent this in the future?"

"You prevent it by asking for boxes," Edward said as he entered the room. "We'll call it my fault. I was in a hurry to get everything here as quickly as possible."

"How can we 'elp?" Lawrence asked.

"Actually," Brown said, "if you can organize those things we had before yesterday, I believe Cadet Peterson and I can have this sorted by midday."

"Very good then, we'll get on with that." Lawrence took a deep breath and walked to the earlier piles of paperwork.

Edward donned white cotton gloves and picked up one of the rifles from Wilford Davis' safe.

"A Gevär försöksmodell 1892," Edward said. "I didn't think the Norwegians released this yet."

"They didn't," Cadet Brown said. "It's not supposed to be released until June. Hence, the designator 1892."

"Our Mister Davis seems to have connections," Franklin said.

"Indeed," Edward said. "6.5 millimeters. Good to 500 meters."

"900," Cadet Brown interrupted.

"You a weapons expert, too, Cadet Brown?"

"I dabble." He returned to his piles of papers.

"Dabble, my arse," Cadet Peterson said. "Sir, he is the best man with a weapon I have seen, including the so-called experts at the academy."

"Then we'll reserve the weapons inspection to our newly-found weapons expert." Edward placed the rifle back on the table.

"The danger, Detective Willoughby," Cadet Brown continued without looking up from his work, "is that the bullet is faster than the speed of sound. The slug would hit its mark two seconds before you would hear the report of the rifle. Theoretically, if the shooter is sure of his shot, and if he's a professional, he would be, he would take down his weapon and be hidden from view before you would be able to look for him."

"A dangerous weapon indeed," Edward muttered.

* * * * *

The work proceeded well. Piles of information were organized into file boxes, the boxes labeled and placed onto the gray shelves.

"Coffee boxes?" Peterson said, looking at the trademark on a brown box. "I thought we would have something made to handle these documents."

"Compile everything in chronological order,"Edward said, "and track clients. As you indicated, many clients have used Wilford's services more than once.

We need to correlate that information with crimes, solved and unsolved."

"Should we concentrate on matching Mister Davis's clients with the Garment Seven?" Cadet Brown suggested.

"I would keep a broader mind regarding our private investigator." Edward looked at the stacks of documents surrounding him. "He has many clients, and his work will not be limited to the garment industry. Perhaps he has legitimate customers."

"Yessir," Cadet Peterson said. "We follow the evidence."

"Wherever it takes us," Cadet Brown added.

* * * * *

Coroner Waddington straightened his lab coat and returned his spectacles to the bridge of his nose. They had been perched atop his head for the past three hours, as he wrote the necropsy for Wilford Davis.

He began with the inventory, which was on his person when the body arrived at Scotland Yard:

"Let's begin with the overcoat first.

"Pipe, Meerschaum, nondescript.

"Pouch, tobacco. Contents…" He emptied the pouch onto a tray, which revealed only tobacco. "Pouch is heavy by itself…hullo…something is sewn into the fabric." He retrieved a sharp blade from his medical kit, and sliced open the leather wall of the pouch. He fished out some coins. "Four gold sovereigns," he muttered, "emergency cash. Not a bad idea."

"Envelope, thick with bills. Counting…five thousand pounds sterling."

"Wallet, with calling cards for Wilford Davis and Harold Lawton. Counting money…thirty three pounds sterling."

"Notebook. Last entry: EW, dead and soon. Public and brutal."

"EW?" the coroner scratched his red beard. "Edward Willoughby?" He turned pale and clutched the notebook to his chest as he locked his office, then ran down the hall. He poked his head inside the staging area for the murder investigation.

"Where's Willoughby?" the panicked scientist gasped.

"Upstairs in his office, but he…"

"Thank you." Waddington ran toward the stairs and almost reached the handrail when he ran into Edward.

"Edward, thank god you're safe." Coroner Waddington gasped for air.

"Coroner Waddington," Edward said, gripping the man's left shoulder. Lawrence held the right. "Sir, you need to slow down."

"I have something of vital importance," he breathed.

"Very well, sir." Edward looked around. "Let's discuss it in the vault."

Thirteen

"So you already knew there was a threat on your life?" Coroner Waddington cleaned his glasses for the tenth time.

"Yessir." Edward studied the unflappable scientist. "But the situation has probably been taken care of."

"In what way?"

"Our killer, Ronald Alexander, killed the contract killer and Harold Lawton, who hired him." Edward showed Waddington the ledger entry.

"Very well." Waddington studied the large pages. "That doesn't mean there won't be another attempt."

"True. My entire team, except the cadets, are now armed." Edward pulled his Bulldog out for emphasis.

"That still does not give me a great deal of confidence."

"Remember old Wallace, at the academy?"

"Yes, I believe we both attended his funeral, five years past."

"We did. Well, Mister Wallace once told me that you can tell you're getting close to your man, as evidenced by him getting desperate."

"Attempted murder of a policeman is certainly desperate."

"Contract killers are a very small community," Edward continued. "I believe Ronald Alexander is looking out for me."

"How can you be certain?"

"We can't, entirely. However, it's obvious he wants me on the case. I believe he would do what ever is necessary to make that happen. The death of this contract killer and the man who hired him demonstrate that."

"Very well, Edward. Be vigilant, just in case." Coroner Waddington stepped toward the door.

"Always, sir."

"My necropsies should be complete by the end of the day." He whisked down the hallway to the morgue.

"I've ne're seen that man so concerned for another, Edward," Lawrence commented. "Ye must be the son 'e ne're 'ad."

"Perhaps, Lawrence. Perhaps." Edward's eyes followed Waddington, until he disappeared around the corner. His face softened, almost to the point of wistfulness. *Well I'll be…*

* * * * *

The task of organization was complete by mid-afternoon, and a break was ordered by Edward. They all sat back with a cup of tea and a biscuit.

Edward looked around the room at the mounds of paper. His eyes came to rest on the most recent stack the cadets had completed. The edges of the paper seemed dirty somehow. *No…wait,* Edward thought. He walked toward the stack, and turned his head sidewise. He picked up the paper and tamped it smooth. He then flared the edges. His eyes lit up, and he retrieved his pen and notebook.

"Find something, Edward?" Franklin said.

"Tell me what you see." Edward pointed at the edge of the stack.

"Words. A code?"

"Fore-edge writing. I have seen these as fore edge paintings on book edges. In this case, words. An index? A message? Either way, we need to translate it," Edward said.

"A code," Peterson said. "I've heard of the Masons using something similar."

"The Masons have dozens of codes," Edward said, continuing to write. "This may be just one of them."

"You a Mason, detective?" Brown said.

"I'll neither confirm nor deny it." Edward smiled.

"Now 'e's just bein' difficult," Lawrence said. "Just because 'e can."

"The words are slightly incomplete," Edward said. "Meaning some of this volume is elsewhere. Our organization of the documents is flawed. We need to integrate the proper pages into this volume, and remove the pages which do not match. More work, gents."

"Aw," Peterson said. "Just when we thought we were close to being finished."

"I believe the tossing of Wilford Davis' office was partially to jumble the information," Edward said, "to make it more difficult for us to diagnose.

"This is not going anywhere, gents. Let's take the evening off, and get back to this in the morning." Edward looked at his exhausted team. "Can ye hear it? The Bull and Castle calls. First round is on me. Cadet Brown, be a good lad and inform Abigail where we will be, lest Coroner Waddington have a coronary. Oh, he's invited as well."

"Straight away sir," Brown grabbed his coat and dashed toward the morgue.

* * * * *

The early crowd at the "Bull and Castle" was limited to a few law enforcement types who worked odd shifts, so finding a large empty table was no problem. The barmaid approached with a towel in hand.

"A round of Arf and Arfs, Juliet," Edward said.

"Certainly, Edward." She fished a piece of paper from her apron. "I took this from an elegant lady yesterday. She didn't want to leave it, but I guaranteed you'd get it." Juliet handed the envelope to Edward.

"Wait." Franklin intercepted the paper. "It might be dangerous." He sniffed it and closed his eyes. "Definitely a refined woman. Wait, let me guess: tall, black, coifed hair, a heart-stopper, with a Russian accent?"

"Why, yes. That'd be her."

"Valeryia," everyone except Edward said, in the same voice.

"Thank you gents very much," Edward said, snatching the envelope from Franklin's grip. He unsealed the flap and retrieved the note, taking care that no one else would see its contents:

Edward,

I hope this finds you well. I just heard you are in danger. A hired killer is after you. Please be careful.

Valeriya.

"Who's Valeriya?" Coroner Waddington said.

"She owns a private club. It was partially through 'er 'elp that we returned to Sunninghill." Edward smiled. "It might seem, sir, that half of London knows of the contract on my life. Juliet, Coroner Waddington's money is no good here. His drink goes on my bill."

"Thank you," Waddington said, snatching the note from Edward's hand. He scanned it. "It might be beneficial for you to thank the lady in person."

"Is everyone trying to push me out the door?" Edward looked around the table, as everyone stared back at him.

"Yes." They all said together.

"Very well," Edward said. "Bring the first round, Juliet."

"Shall I ring for Charlie Wolverstein? Say, half an hour?" Juliet winked.

"That will do nicely," Edward said.

"Charlie who?" Waddington said.

"Cabbie," Andreason said. "He found out we're honest coppers, and gives us a discount."

* * * * *

Franklin and Lawrence looked in every direction and stepped to the curb first. Edward slid into the seat, and Franklin handed the address to Charlie.

"Thank ye, Franklin. Detective Willoughby, do ye wish me to wait for ye?"

"No, thank you Charlie," Edward said. "I might be a while. When you return here, though, I'm certain some of my mates might need a lift. Let's be off to Wandsworth."

* * * * *

The fog blew across the street, limiting vision to less than twenty feet. Water coated the city and dripped from everything. The sign for the club was almost invisible. Edward fished out the cryptic membership card for this exclusive gentlemen's club.

The same guard from two weeks past greeted Edward and scarcely looked at the three stones and calling card. He motioned him through with barely a glance.

"Hey!" a patron in line called to the guard. "You didn't even check his card."

"That's because 'e's privledged." He winked at Edward. "Have a nice day."

Edward tipped his hat and entered the opulence inside.

Fourteen

"She's looking for you sir," an attractive hostess said to Edward, as she took his coat, hat and scarf. "I'll let her know you're here. There are plenty of refreshments in the next room."

"Thank you," Edward said and stepped up to the bar. The heavy carpets were welcome comfort to his tired feet, and he choose to stand at the end of the bar until Valeriya's arrival. He placed his hands on the engraved copper surface of the bar, marveling at its craftsmanship.

"What'll ya have?" The bartender was male, early thirties, well-dressed with a wrinkled smile. His sculptured mutton chops framed his round face. He had a tie and a red silk vest, and matching red garters decorated his upper arms.

"Scotch, neat."

"We have several kinds of scotch, sir."

"He'll have the thirty-year-old Macallan," a familiar woman's voice said from behind. "And he pays for nothing here."

"Yes, miss," he said and reached for the afore-mentioned bottle.

"Valeriya," Edward said.

"Edward," Valeriya answered. She threw her arms around him and hugged him far longer than a normal greeting would take. "I was worried about you," she whispered into his ear.

"It seems I have a guardian angel," He smiled at her. He noted her perfect skin once more. Her beauty swept over him.

She picked up two crystal glasses from the bar and handed one to Edward. "Shall we?" She slipped her arm in his and led him upstairs to a private room. The walls were lined with red velvet drapes, and embroidered tapestries with Russian scenery and stories. A cocktail table sat in the center of the room and a divan figured prominently on the far wall. She motioned to the small sofa, and followed him across the room.

He sat, not certain how comfortable to make himself. She seated herself closer than a lady might, and crossed her legs. Edward felt himself flush.

"Am I too close?" Valeriya said.

"In any setting but this one, perhaps," Edward said. She started shift away from him when he took her hand. "But I can get used to your proximity."

"I was hoping you would say that," she said. "I am not versed in the ways of being a lady. Perhaps you could help me with them."

"Perhaps," Edward studied her. "Perhaps we could help each other."

"How so?"

"I come from culture, but not money," he said. "Therefore, I am acquainted with societal norms. I can help you there, and perhaps you could help me understand your heritage."

"Are you certain you want to understand?"

"If it involves you, I want to understand." *Damn!* He thought. *That was almost giving away too much.*

"It may take a while." Her perfume was intoxicating. "And you are trying to catch a killer."

"I'm always trying to catch a killer. But they rarely try and kill me."

"You said you have a guardian angel?"

"Oh, yes." He debated how much to tell her. "Of course, this is hush-hush."

"Of course."

"It seems the man I am pursuing murdered both the contract killer and the man who hired him."

"Why would he do that?"

"He and I had an encounter seven years past. He wants only me on the case."

"Why?"

"It's complicated, and until we complete the case, the rest must be kept secret."

"I understand. As long as you're safe, I shan't bother you with questions."

"Thank you. And thank you for the warning."

"It seems you already knew the threat."

"I appreciate your concern, nonetheless."

"You know, Edward, you did not need to come in person to thank me."

"You came in person to warn me." Edward realized he was still holding her hand. He stared at her delicate features for a moment. "This is most comfortable."

"It is indeed."

They shared the throat-warming scotch, staring at their own glasses. Neither wanted to break the silence, yet each knew that one of them should say something. It was quiet in the room, the bar noises below almost non-existent.

"About your customs, Valeriya," Edward said. "What would they be for an event involving thirty year aged alcohol?"

"Na zda-ró-vye!" she said, hoisting her glass above them both.

"Na zda-ró-vye!" Edward said, repeating the gesture. "See? I'm learning already."

Fifteen

The noise of the crowded bar had faded into the distance, and the cigar smoke was non-existent. Edward felt his body, now covered in pajamas not his. The night wear bore a soft elegance, encouraging him to stay in bed. He opened one eye to see both of Valeria's wonderful ice blue pools staring back at him.

"Good morning," he said.

"And good morning to you," Valeriya said, her soft voice just above a whisper. "I was going to wake you soon. I'm certain your fellow policemen will be concerned if you are late."

"They will be," he said and propped himself up on the thick array of pillows. He felt the silk sheets between his fingers. "You have excellent taste in adornments." He glanced about the room, noting the expensive vanity, drapes, and bed.

"I would expect your residence would be nicely appointed as well," she said.

"That would be attributed to my late aunt. It was her hand which splashed grace across my residence."

"Then you must invite me for a visit, so I can see what your late aunt has wrought. Tea?" She motioned to a serving tray with a teapot, fruit and pastries.

"Yes, and yes," he said, a tiny smile forming. *Why does this feel so comfortable?*

"I will hurry you along, then, Edward, to keep both our days moving forward."

* * * * *

"Do I detect a bit of a lift in your step, Detective Willoughby?" Detective Sergeant Johnson peered over the top of his square reading glasses. His elevated position behind the duty desk projected the appearance of power.

"Perhaps," Edward said, "It's a lovely day, is it not?"

"It's raining like cats and dogs, it is. Wot's gotten into ya?"

"I believe the good detective's in the hands of Saint Valentine." Lawrence slapped a hand on Edward's shoulder. "He's wearing the same clothes as yesterday, and…" Lawrence sniffed Edward's collar."…the scent of Valeriya Tatyana Kipriyanov. Aye, my dear Detective Sergeant Johnson, the laddie's in love."

"With a Russian goddess, no less," Franklin said, shaking his soaked umbrella as he entered the lobby. "We should all be so lucky."

"Then I'll hold you gents responsible to keep Edward focused. The cases before you are already complex enough. Thankfully there are no new developments this morning, yet. Off you go."

* * * * *

Cadets Brown and Peterson were already hard at work, organizing the stacks of documents, so the message for each volume would manifest itself. The number of piles of documents had grown from the initial dozen to nearly thirty.

The three detectives and one bobby stood at the door and watched the two young men labor like a single machine. They talked little, a single word here and there. Each carried a sheaf of papers, and compared the flared edges of each stack of documents, inserting an appropriate page in a specific stack. They moved like lightning, and did not even notice they had an audience.

"They look like the soldiers on a clockwork, don't they?" Abigail Etherington said, looking over their shoulders. "They've been at this since before I arrived, which was early. I'm not certain they left the building."

"They most certainly left they building," Edward said. "We all took part in depleting the stock of ale at the Bull and Castle this night last."

"Some of us more than others," Lawrence added. He nodded at Edward.

"Did ya not stay until the end, Edward?" She leaned closer and sniffed. "Do I detect perfume?"

"You are most observant, Abigail," Edward said. "I'll update you when it's convenient."

"Oh, it's convenient right now," Lawrence said. "Don't even bother the two lads right now. I've not see such coordination before. Let 'em finish with the project."

Abigail began to drag Edward toward the mortuary. He looked back at the evidence room.

"We've got this, Edward," Robert Andreason said. "I'll let you know when they finish."

"See? They have this." Abigail said, her eyes twinkling. "Now, who's this woman you obviously spent the night with?" They strolled toward her huge desk.

* * * * *

"So, did ya…" Abigail whispered. "Ya know…"

"I know what you're asking, Abigail," Edward said and rubbed his sore temples. "Truth be told, I can't remember."

"Oh my…you know, as difficult and embarrassing as this might seem, you have to ask her."

"And inform her that I can't remember the most important event of a relationship?"

"Yes."

"Perhaps I'll wait until we've had such an encounter that I can remember."

"Don't worry, Edward," Robert said, placing a comforting hand on his shoulder. "It 'appens. And your secret is safe with me."

"Thank you," Edward said. "I take it our two cadets are finished?"

"They are. You need to see the results."

"Thank you for listening, Abigail," Edward said, and picked up his notebook.

"Any time," Abigail said. "Now off with you."

* * * * *

The stacks had not gotten thinner, as hoped. The number had grown to over forty. Peterson and Brown sat on two chairs behind the tables. They stared as though seeing far away.

"I wouldn't bother them just yet, Edward," Lawrence said. "When I was in Crimea and we had constant contact with the enemy, our frontline soldiers developed what we called the 'thousand yard stare.' Give 'em a few minutes to come out of it."

"If they take an hour to recover, they're still the fastest, best-suited blokes for that kind of a job," Edward said, looking at the stacks. *There must be five or six thousand individual pages here.* He studied their faces. The young men seemed to not even be aware of their surroundings.

The minutes passed with a pace similar to watching two slugs pursue a rogue leaf. The detectives paced, stood on one leg, then the other, but did not interrupt Cadets Brown and Peterson.

Peterson stirred first. He looked down at his cold tea, then nudged Brown, who looked at his friend.

They both stood, stretched and looked at Edward and the rest of the policemen on "the team."

"Thank you for being patient with us."

"We are going to need the files on all unsolved murders involving gunfire for the past ten years," Peterson said. "There are forty seven piles here. Forty seven cases."

"Before you go any farther," Edward said, "I need to have you explain this to someone else. Take a quick rest, collect your thoughts. Ensure you brief us quickly, yet thoroughly upon my return."

Edward raced up to the fourth floor. He returned five minutes later with a tall gentleman, in a white shirt and a dark gray tie. Broad suspenders supported his trousers, and he sported a large, thick mustache. A cigar hung from his right hand.

"Gentlemen, I am Superintendent McCarthy." A smile formed as he studied the reaction of the two cadets as to who they would be briefing. "I understand you have uncovered far-reaching evidence."

"We...uh have, sir," Peterson said.

"It involves as many as forty seven murders," Brown added.

"Going back as far as ten years," Peterson said.

"Very well," McCarthy said. "Show us what you have, and we'll decide how to proceed."

"Yessir," Brown said. He pointed to the closest stack of papers. "Note the edge code on this stack. It is entitled 'Tweed. 16-4-89. Wandsworth.' I believe that to be either the hiree or the victim with the name of Tweed, sixteen March, 1889, in Wandsworth, London."

"That'd be Russell Tweed," Lawrence said. "I was assigned that case. Never found the killer."

"Excellent," Peterson said, writing on a plain piece of paper, which he placed on the stack. "Now, for the details. At the top of certain pages are a series of numbers. In this case, on these pages, is the following information:

16. 10-1-1 = C
17. 5-4-1 = a
19. 5-5-3 = s

"I won't bore you with the details, sirs," Peterson said, "but it's an Ottendorf cipher. The key is the only item which did not fit with the rest of the safe: Sonnets From the Portugese. Poem 16, third line, second word, first character of that word. We need to translate each of these stacks, which will most likely detail who hired Mister Davis, for which job, and how much he was paid."

"How long to decipher the code?" Superintendent said, fingering his mustache.

"Not long sir," Brown said. "Tomorrow, at the latest."

"Excellent," McCarthy said. "Edward, it seems your team has its direction. Let me know when you are ready to proceed."

"Yes, sir," Edward said.

McCarthy puffed on his cigar as he trotted back upstairs.

"Well," Edward said, "let's get busy and see if we can translate all of the Davis files before we go home tonight."

Sixteen

The Bull and Castle was abuzz with policemen from both Scotland Yard and every station within five miles. Only one table remained with available chairs, occupied by a rotund red-headed, red-bearded man. He looked like he could occupy almost any door, thus preventing the escape of fleeing felons.

"Sam," Edward said, walking directly toward the man. Sam knocked his chair over, almost falling in the process. Only a quick response from Edward saved him from tumbling into a large group of detectives standing behind the table.

"Oh, Lordy," Lawrence said, his voice directed at the cadets.

"What goes, Griffin?" Brown said.

"Now we'll have to 'ear again about how Sam single-handedly saved London from gangsters." Lawrence sighed. "And he's already had more than one pint."

"But we'll have a place to sit, right?" Peterson noted.

"Might not be worth it," Franklin interjected. "Well, Edward seems charitable this evening, so we'll 'umor him."

Lawrence and Franklin put on their professional smiles and shook hands with Sam.

"And these fine upstanding gentlemen are Andreason, Brown and Peterson," Franklin said. "The order is alphabetical, not in rank order, nor by age."

"Niesh to meet ya all," Sam said, then looked at Cadet Brown. "Say, didn't I meet ya the last time Willoughby was 'ere thish late?"

"Yes, Sam, you did. And you admonished me to only use last names in this fine establishment. Say, is Sam your last name?"

"Why, no, laddie 'tisn't. It's me first name. I'm a wee bit Sco'ish, and no one can e'er remember me last name, so Sam it is."

So, then Sam," Peterson said, "What exactly is your surname?"

"Farquharson, F-A-R-Q-U-H-A-R-S-O-N," Sam said. "Remember, it's pronounced FARKERSHEN, not the many variations the lowly Englanders try."

"I'm Peterson, and this cretin is Brown. Nice to meetcha, Mister Farkershen," Peterson extended his hand.

"And nice to meet ye both." Sam's hand engulfed Peterson's. "Oh, if yer lookin' for me in this establishment, it's just Sam."

"Good to know, Sam."

"Well, Sam," Edward said, "For letting us sit with you, I'll buy you a pint of 'arf and 'arf."

"You're a fine one, you are, Willoughby." Sam drained the beer in front of him and waving toward the waitress. "Rebecca, my dear lady, Mister Willoughby here has been kind enough to purchase another ale for me."

"Coming right up," Rebecca said. The waitress gave Edward a stern look, and he responded with a "what was I supposed to do?" expression of his own. The policemen then chatted regarding topics such as sports, various stock exchanges, and local news.

It was after ten o'clock and Sam's head had begun to droop. "Sam," Peterson said, "I believe we should call ye a cab."

"Perhaps, lad, perhaps," Sam said. "Waddya think, Willoughby?"

"I believe it's best, Sam," Edward said, "especially if you want to get anything done tomorrow."

"Verrry well, " Sam said, and stood. Only by holding the table was he able to stay vertical, and he struggled to put on his overcoat. The cadets aided in getting the massive garment on Sam's right arm. Franklin then held that arm, keeping Sam upright, while the they finished the job of positioning the greatcoat on Sam's large frame.

Franklin buttoned the coat while Andreason kept the him standing. Peterson's face showed concern as he placed Sam's bowler on his matted hair. Ready.

"I've got ye a cab, Sam," Lawrence said as he walked through the pub's door. All five men slowly navigated their way outside into the rainy night. Edward stayed at the table, keeping it safe for his team.

"Ya got his Ps and Qs, Rebecca?" Edward said.

"Only pints this night," she said, her dark brown hair falling in the path of her notes.

"So, 'ow's he doin'?"

"Total, or just this evening?"

"Total."

"Twenty three pints."

"And food?"

"Are ye gonna cover 'is expenses again, Edward?" Rebecca looked at the blackboard ledger behind the bar.

"Just how much?"

"A pound and a crown."

Edward placed three coins in her delicate hand. "And a crown for you, young lady."

"Why do ye do this?"

"Because no one else will."

"You know huggin' is forbidden by me boss, Edward," she said.

"Then I'll take a magical hug, Rebecca." He reached up and wiped a tear from her left eye. "Now, off you go, lest your patrons get loud." She turned back toward the bar. As she passed the blackboard, she erased the tally next to Sam's name.

Brown and Peterson plopped down in their chairs, opposite Edward. They sipped their beers for a few moments.

"How about the London Exchange?" Peterson said.

"Yes," Brown answered, "do ya really think there'll be a panic?"

"Probably," Edward said. "Remember, it's all about perception. The important thing to remember is patience. Regardless of what transpires, in five or so years it will appear as though nothing happened. It does not lessen the impact today, however. Those who panic and pull their money out of the banks will probably suffer.

"I have an ample stock of silver and cash in my own safe deposit box. Courtesy of my late great aunt, of course. So, I'm not worried, one way or the other."

"Of course," both cadets said together.

"You two do that a lot," Andreason said.

"What's that?" The two cadets said.

"You say things exactly. Together."

"We've noticed," Brown said.

"We also don't know what to do about it," Peterson said.

"I say you do nothing," Edward said, taking another bite of his sandwich. "It actually gives me faith that ye believe what you're saying. Oh, and we don't talk about the Davis findings outside Scotland Yard."

"Yessir," they said as one.

Seventeen

Murders. Contract Killings. Assassinations. Mercy killings. More than six per year for a dozen years. Eighty-three all told.

Maimings. Retribution beatings. Abusive husbands with broken hands, legs and deformed body parts. Fathers who beat their children, who beat them no more. Persons who disappeared with no trace. Thieves who left their victims penniless gave back what they stole. All of these afraid to commit the same offense again. Ever. There were too many of these to count.

Each one unsolved.

Piles of documents filled the tables in the room. Each stack was arranged by date, separated in six-month increments.

"We may have as many as four hundred cases here," Lawrence said. "How are we going to solve so many?"

"Concentrate on the murders," Edward said. "If the rest of the 'victims' are afraid to be criminals, I am comfortable in letting them remain as they are."

"Was Wilford Davis some sort of Robin Hood?" Peterson said. "He used the contract killings to finance a campaign against crime in London?"

"It seems so," Edward said, scratching behind his ear. He raised his voice so everyone could hear him. "Everyone, let's not lessen the damage he has done to the community. For the present, let's concentrate on the eighty-plus murders. If crime is deterred by the lack of resolution of Mister Davis' other crimes, we *may* be less aggressive in those cases. As I already stated, concentrate on the homicides, first and foremost.

"Start with the most recent, and work backward. These will be active cases, with current supporting evidence, and the easiest to solve. Anything older than five years will belong to my cold case people upstairs."

"So, let's get busy on the past six months, then the six months before that, and so on?" Andreason asked.

"Yes," Edward replied. "That would be a good strategy. Remember, we already know who committed the crime. We want the person who hired Mister Davis. Also, place garment industry cases in a single group."

Everyone took parts of the most recent Davis clients, sifting through the events. A blank paper was clipped to the top sheet of each stack, to hold the information. Dates were checked, and cases cross-referenced. The capitol offences were completed by the end of the second day, and the next morning the team began delivering the information to the lead detective in each case.

The Garment Factory cases amounted to more than two each year. It was a steady income for Wilford Davis, as his fee for each deed was £10,000. The team would have plenty to do for the next few months.

The hallway was dark when Edward and Lawrence closed the heavy doors to the former evidence room. The clicking of the locking pins of the door echoed down the deserted hall.

"Lord lumme," Lawrence said, "another note." He reached for the white envelope stuck to the door.

"Wait, Lawrence," Edward said, reaching inside his brief case and retrieving a pair of tongs. "Use these."

"Thank you," Lawrence said, and took the tool in his left hand. He pulled the envelope free and read the outer flap.

"It's for you," and handed the tongs to Edward, who opened it. The note inside read:

```
Detective Willoughby:
Concentrate on JE, HW and LS.
Plenty of evidence there.
```

"Alright," Lawrence said, "I get HW and LS. That'd be Harley Winthorpe and Langley Smythe, but who's JE?"

"Open up the vault," Robert said. "I have an idea."

Edward twisted the key in the lock and pulled the two doors open. Robert strode to the ledger and ran his fingers down the columns of figures.

"See here." His voice contained excitement. "A note on the left, followed by a note on the right, outside of the columns. 'J' on the left and 'E' on the right. Dozens and dozens of entries. These make no sense, until you put it all together. 'JE' is not a *who*, it's a *what*."

"But what?" Franklin scratched his red beard.

"What company stands to profit from the garment industry?"

"Jameson Engineering," Edward said. "They make the machines for the garment industry."

"We must tread lightly until we're certain," Edward said. "Jameson is powerful and ruthless. It is possible we would all be in danger if we tip our hand too early. No. We confirm the evidence first."

Edward locked the vault door behind them. *We're going to take on the fifth most powerful man in England,* thought Edward. *We'd better be right. Our careers, and our very lives, may depend upon it.*

* * * * *

Edward breathed a sigh of relief as he turned toward Whitehall Place, the street in front of Scotland Yard. The vault was safely locked, and his team was heading home. He jammed his hands into his pockets and studied the fog that he breathed into the night air. *It looks almost like a small steam engine,* he thought.

The detective strolled among the trees along the Thames. He was unaware of his surroundings as he reviewed the events of the day. The icy wind blowing across water of the river washed his soul, ridding it of the foul deeds of others.

He paused to light his pipe, and observed the movement of the few barges being pushed about by tugs at this late hour. *We'll solve these outstanding cases. I am confident of that. But more pressing than that is Ronald Alexander. We must pinch that bugger, and soon.*

* * * * *

The barrel of the rifle rested on a sandbag in the second floor window. The shooter trained his telescopic sight across the Thames River, on the illuminated man puffing on a pipe in front of the red brick building. It mattered little that the structure was Scotland Yard, and the target was a detective. A contract was a contract.

A practiced finger wrapped around the front trigger. The detective moved down the street, to the right. The front trigger clicked.

The pressure increased on the second trigger.

* * * * *

A shadow moved behind the shooter, and a flashing blade did its work.

A different man looked through the sight, watching Edward Willoughby as he strolled home.

"Rest well, Edward," the man said. "Rest well."

ABOUT THE AUTHOR

Tim Lewis is a former U.S. Navy Journalist and reporter for a small weekly newspaper. He has been writing for most of his adult life, but literary accomplishments have come within the past few years. He has many works in progress in several genres, and Murder in Dartmouth Park is his third novella in the Edward Willoughby series.

Look for Murder on the Docks, coming soon.

www.ingramcontent.com/pod-product-compliance
Lightning Source LLC
Chambersburg PA
CBHW070535130626
46555CB00003B/1431